The 'E' Book

The 'E' Book

Essential prayers and activities
for faith at home

Gill Ambrose

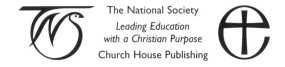

The National Society
*Leading Education
with a Christian Purpose*
Church House Publishing

National Society/Church House Publishing
Church House
Great Smith Street
London SW1P 3NZ

ISBN 0 7151 4937 7

Published 2000 by the National Society (Church of England) for Promoting Religious Education and Church House Publishing.

Cover design by Stuart Squires, SGA

Printed in England by The Cromwell Press Ltd, Trowbridge, Wiltshire

Contents

Contents

Foreword

I was brought up with family prayers at the breakfast table, and in due course introduced our offspring to the same practice. But then both my father and grandfather were clergymen. Resources and the confidence to deploy them were to hand. But how is it for the vast majority of families?

This book, which grew out of a conversation in Ely between Gill Ambrose and myself, is intended to meet an increasingly obvious need in our age. Prayer has to be re-established at home, as a normal, domestic activity. Participating in fun activities related to the church's year, and in that context offering straightforward prayers, is a vital way of helping to root children in God's time. Advent, Christmas, Epiphany, Easter, Ascension and Pentecost plus a generous sprinkling of Saints' days give a sense of depth and transcendence to the natural turn of the seasons, and the rhythms of the week. In this way children and their parents will discover God accompanying them on their journey through life and be refreshed and encouraged in surprising ways.

We need to talk about God with children. This highly recommended book will enable adults to do so with confidence, and have fun in the process.

Rt Revd Professor Stephen W Sykes

Principal, St John's College, Durham

February 2000

Acknowledgements

The inspiration for this book was the concern of Bishop Stephen Sykes, then Bishop of Ely, to find ways of supporting Christian families in their everyday lives. A small group of people came together to try and work out what could be provided that would be usable, family-friendly and rooted in Christian tradition. I am grateful to all those who gave considerable time and energy to wrestling with this. Diana Osborn generously shared many ideas in the early stages. Jane Keiller and Jackie Cray wrote the first drafts of fifteen of the chapters and were closely involved in the generation of many of the others and in determining the overall content. I am grateful to them all for the energy they put into the development of this book.

The author and publisher gratefully acknowledge permission to reproduce copyright material in this publication. Every effort has been made to trace and contact copyright holders. If there are any inadvertent omissions we apologize to those concerned and will ensure that a suitable acknowledgement is made at the next reprint. Page numbers are indicated in parentheses.

American Bible Society: extracts from the *Good News Bible,* published by the Bible Societies and HarperCollins Publishers, are copyright © American Bible Society 1994 and are used with permission.

Christian Aid: for the prayer by Janet Morley, © Christian Aid, 1999. Used with permission. **(48)**

Hodder & Stoughton Ltd: excerpts from the *Holy Bible, New International Version.* Copyright © 1973, 1978, 1984 by International Bible Society. Used by permission of Hodder & Stoughton, a member of the Hodder Headline Group. All rights reserved. 'NIV' is a trademark of International Bible Society. UK trademark number 1448790.

International Commission on English in the Liturgy: the English translation of the Easter Proclamation (*Exsultet*) from *Rite of Holy Week* © 1972, International

Introduction

This book of ideas for getting to know God better has been created for ordinary families by ordinary families. Here are things to do together which will help us to search for and know God. This is what Christians call prayer. Throughout human time, people have looked for God and found ways to draw close to God. One great Christian writer, St Augustine, described this search very beautifully in the words 'our hearts are restless till they find their rest in you'.

When we think of prayer, we often think of lots of complicated words and church services, of being very still and silent. But for small children, who can only be still and silent for a very short time, prayer – searching for God – will be learnt as much in what they do as in what they say. We all learn best by experience, and this is particularly true for young children. All the *essentials* in *The 'E' Book* are meant for children and parents to do together. The language used throughout the book is deliberately simple and direct, so that older children can read the suggestions and perhaps lead the family, or younger sisters and brothers, in some of the activities that are suggested. Everything is designed to be done in and around the home, or on family outings or holidays. The home and the family is the first and primary place of learning for young children, and even when children start school, the home remains an important place of discovery.

The collection of ideas has been drawn together from the experience of several families who have been happy to share things that they have done which have become family traditions. But very many of the suggestions are much older than us. They have developed over two thousand years of Christian history and beyond and represent some its greatest riches. Because we have tried them out, however, we are confident that families today will enjoy trying them too. We have also found that they have grown with us. Some ideas, especially those for Christmas and Easter, grew as our children grew. Some of the suggestions in the book are suitable only for very small children, others will be rather too complicated until children are well into the years at school. So we hope that *The 'E' Book* will grow with your family, and that eventually this book will wear out. By that time, however, the activities you have grown to love will be so much part of your life that you won't need the book anymore.

xi

How to use *The 'E' Book*

The pattern of Christian worship follows the natural seasons of the year. This works well in the northern hemisphere and provides us with ready-made symbols. So we celebrate the birth of Jesus, the light of the world, in the darkest month at Christmas. In the spring, with new life bursting everywhere from the ground, we celebrate God overcoming death with the Resurrection of Jesus.

The 'E' Book follows the months of the year and provides about four ideas for each month. Around Advent and Christmas, and Lent and Easter, there are some ideas that can be used every day. For the rest of the year, there is about one idea a week. Sometimes these are for a particular day, perhaps a saint's day, and the date is given. Other pages simply have an idea that is appropriate for the time of year. There are quite a lot of summer holiday ideas that could be used in July or August, whenever you can make the time available. At the end we provide some general suggestions and ideas: bedtime prayers, famous prayers and ideas about good books.

Pages v and vi include an *essentials* calendar of the months and seasons and a list of the things that there are to do throughout the year. The calendar runs from January to December, but you can start anytime. And you do not need to use every idea. Some will be good for little children, others will be better for older ones. Your children may not be old enough for some of our suggestions yet. Or they may already be too old for some things. You are meant to pick and choose. There is probably too much for most people to manage in a year. However, *The 'E' Book* is meant to last! We hope that some of these activities will become part of your family tradition and that they will grow and change with you, just as they have grown and changed down the ages.

January and February

New Year's Day: 1 January

The New Year TV schedules usually feature lots of programmes looking back over the significant events of the last twelve months. In more recent years, as we have moved into the new millennium, we looked back over the last decade, the last century and the last thousand years as well. It is important to look back, to see what has been achieved, and what lessons can be learnt. But it is important to look forward also, to try and plan to do better.

In some old churches and cathedrals you can see paintings and carvings of a calendar of the months: the series of twelve pictures shows what happened during each month of the year. In June the hay was harvested, in July the corn. In September you picked the grapes, and so on. Most of the scenes depicted are agricultural (though in May the farmer is sometimes shown going to war on his horse) but January always shows a person (sometimes said to be the Roman god Januarius) with two heads, looking in opposite directions, sometimes through two doors. The two-headed person is looking back over the old year that has just concluded, and forward into the new year.

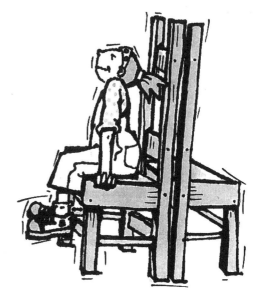

You could play an *Old Year, New Year* game, inspired by this January picture. You can't develop two heads, but you could put two chairs back to back and in turn sit on the one which looks back over the year that has just gone and then move round to the other looking forward into the new year. On the looking back chair, each person can give thanks to God for one especially good thing that has happened in the old year, and perhaps one thing they regret. In the new year chair you could say one thing that you are looking forward to and ask for God's help in the year that is just beginning.

A New Year Prayer

Eternal God,
we give you thanks for bringing us
through the changes of time
to the beginning of another year.
Forgive us the wrongs we have done
in the year that is past,
and help us to spend the rest of our days
to your honour and glory;
through Jesus Christ our Lord. Amen.

I am the Alpha and the Omega, the First and the Last, the Beginning and the End.

Revelation 22.13 (NIV)

4

Epiphany: 6 January

This is the day when we celebrate that Jesus was shown to the three wise men, people who were not Jews. It is a sign that God shows his love, not just to his chosen people, but to the whole world. The word Epiphany comes from the Greek word meaning 'to show'. Read the story of the three wise men who followed the star to find Jesus. You can find it in the Bible in St Matthew's Gospel, chapter 2, verses 1 to 2 and 9 to 12.

 In France they make a King's Cake to celebrate Epiphany. A dry bean is baked inside the cake and when the cake is eaten, the person who gets the bean is King. The King can choose a person to be Queen for the rest of the party. Younger children might like to dress up.

You could have a celebration tea party by making a cake and decorating it with a star. A simple way of doing this is to place a star template on top of the cake and sprinkle icing sugar all over the surface. Lift the template off. You could decorate individual biscuits in the same way instead.

You could cover a cardboard star with tinfoil and play Hunt the Star. Toddlers might like to sing '*Twinkle, twinkle special star*.'

When you take your Christmas decorations down, you might like to leave out the crib figures, or at least Jesus and the wise men, until 2 February (see page 11).

A German Epiphany tradition is to bless the house and mark the main doorway with the date of the year that has just begun and a reminder of the journey made by the three wise men whose names, legend says, were Caspar, Melchior and Balthazar. So, for the year 2001, the marking above the door would be 20 C+M+B 01. When the door has been marked a prayer can be said asking God to bless the home and all the journeys that will be made in and out of it during the year.

An Epiphany Prayer

Lord Jesus, as the wise men risked everything to look for you,
help us to seek you in our lives and find your presence with us. Amen.

'*Where is the baby born to be king of the Jews? We saw his star when it came up in the east, and we have come to worship him.*'

Matthew 2.2 (GNB)

Sorting out the Christmas cards: a job for a January day

Knowing what to do with the Christmas cards is always a problem. Do you just put them in the bin? Or find a suitable recycling place? Whatever you finally choose to do with them, you can spend a bit of time, on a day when it's too cold to go out, looking through them to see what you can discover together. Many small children love to sort things and this is an opportunity to develop this skill while exploring Christmas symbols together! It also prolongs Christmas a bit into the days when everything can seem rather flat, when the house is empty again after lots of visitors or trips to visit relatives.

Here are some criteria for sorting your cards. Once you have begun, you will discover between you plenty of others.

* Cards with baby Jesus on and those without

* Cards with camels, shepherds, stars, or angels on (What other categories can you find?)

* Cards with children on. (Talk about what it might have been like to visit the stable and see this special baby. If you had been able to take Jesus a present like the kings did, what would you have taken?)

Perhaps you might like to choose just one card to save and put up on a bedroom wall for a bit, as a reminder that Jesus was once a little person too!

When you finally put the cards away, or take them to be recycled or whatever, you might like to say this prayer together:

Thank you for cards,
Thank you for Christmas,
Thank you for Jesus,
Thank you for love. Amen

Can you add some more thank yous?

There are lots of letters in the Bible and the writers of them usually send their greetings and prayers at the beginning:

May God our Father and the Lord Jesus Christ give you grace and peace. I always give thanks to my God for you because of the grace he has given you through Christ Jesus.

1 Corinthians 1.3-4 (GNB)

Stargazing: an activity
for a clear night

Looking at the stars on a clear, dark night is a wonderful experience that everyone should have.

Choose a clear night and go outside. You see more stars if you can get away from street lighting. Just take your time and look up at the sky. Look for stars that twinkle and see if you can see any of the famous star patterns or constellations. Older children and grown-ups may like to use a book to help find some of the constellations. But just look and wonder. On a really clear night you might see the Milky Way, or you could be lucky enough to see a shooting star.

Some of the people who wrote the Bible were obviously stargazers too. Read some of the 'star writing' in the Bible when you come back in or even take out this book and a torch when you go stargazing.

From Psalm 8 (GNB)

> O Lord, our Lord,
> your greatness is seen in all the world!
> Your praise reaches up to the heavens.
> When I look at the sky, which you have made,
> at the moon and stars, which you set in their places –
> what are human beings, that you think of them;
> mere mortals, that you care for them?

From the Book of Job, chapter 9 (GNB)

No one helped God spread out the heavens
or trample the sea monster's back.
God hung the stars in the sky –
The Great Bear,
Orion, the Pleiades, and the stars of the south.
We cannot understand the great things he does,
and to his miracles there is no end.

From Genesis, chapter 15 (GNB)

Abram heard the Lord speaking to him again:
'Look at the sky and try to count the stars;
you will have as many descendants as that.'

Candlemas: 2 February

Today we remember how Joseph and Mary took baby Jesus to say thank you to God in the Temple in Jerusalem. There they met two old people, Simeon and Hannah. They both saw the baby and said thank you to God for him too. Simeon said that Jesus was like 'a light to reveal God's will to the Gentiles'. You can find his special prayer and the whole story in the Bible, in St Luke's Gospel, chapter 2, verses 22–40.

There is one tradition which suggests that a few figures from the Christmas Crib can be left up after the rest are put away on 6 January, as a reminder of Jesus' childhood. People also light candles on this day to remind them of Simeon's words about Jesus being 'a light'.

 Wrap up the last few crib figures and put them away carefully with the rest.

Put as many candles as you can find in the place where the crib was and use a few bricks or stones to build a little wall around the candles to remind you of the Temple. Take it in turns to light them (you can use one of the candles to light all the others) until they are all lit. Turn the lights out and see how the light from the candles shines out over the wall and can be seen in the whole room. Remember that Jesus' love fills the whole world and can reach everywhere, just like the candle light from inside

the wall. Perhaps a grown-up or an older child can read Simeon's special prayer from St Luke's Gospel.

It's good to make a tradition of getting in touch with grandparents, if you have them, today. If not, perhaps thinking of Simeon and Anna could be a reminder to go and visit an elderly neighbour or friend.

Simeon's Prayer– the Nunc Dimittis

(*Nunc Dimittis* is Latin and means '*Now you can go*'.)

Now, Lord, you have kept your promise,
and you may let your servant go in peace.
With my own eyes I have seen your salvation,
which you have prepared in the presence of all peoples:
A light to reveal your will to the Gentiles
and bring glory to your people Israel.

Luke 2.29-32 (GNB)

6

Building houses:
a fun thing to do on a rainy day

Put some dry sand in a nice tidy heap on a large plate and blow gently across the top of it. (Be careful that it doesn't go into anyone's eyes.) What happens? Tidy the heap again and then pour water on it. If you are happy to go and splash about outside, you could do this with puddle water. See what happens. Play with the wet sand and talk about it.

If it's windy, you could go to a high or exposed place and feel the wind blowing against you. Talk about what that feels like.

Jesus told a story about two men: one built his house on rock and the other built it on sand. You can read the story in St Matthew's Gospel, chapter 7, verses 24 to 27 or in a Children's Bible.

Do you know this song?

The wise man built his house upon the rock (sing 3 times)
And the rains came tumbling down.
The rains came down and the floods came up (sing 3 times)
And the house on the rock stood firm.

The foolish man built his house upon the sand (sing 3 times)
And the rains came tumbling down.
The rains came down and the floods came up (sing 3 times)
And the house on the sand fell flat.

A prayer

Thank you, God, for being our rock,
a safe place when the storms blow in our lives
and times are difficult. Amen.

Something else to do

Colour little piles of fine sand with food colouring and then use them
to make a picture of a house. Stick the sand down with glue.

St Valentine's Day: 14 February

Valentine is said to have been a Roman who was killed because he was a Christian, though no one seems to know very much about what he did. Nor does anyone really know for certain why the day on which he is remembered is marked out as a day for lovers, though some say that it is because this is the earliest day on which birds begin to pair up and mate! However, given that this is the day when the whole world seems to be thinking about love, it seems a good idea to join in! If Valentine gets the credit, that's fine.

One of the most beautiful descriptions of love is found in the Bible in the first letter to the Corinthians, chapter 13. It is often read at weddings and many people know it almost off by heart. Here is part of it:

I may be able to speak the languages of human beings and even of angels, but if I have no love, my speech is no more than a noisy gong or a clanging bell... I may have all the faith needed to move mountains – but if I have no love, I am nothing... Love is patient and kind; it is not jealous or conceited or proud; love is not ill-mannered or selfish or irritable; love does not keep a record of wrongs; love is not happy with evil, but is happy with the truth. Love never gives up; and its faith, hope and patience never fail. (GNB)

A family game to celebrate love

Use one of the symbols associated with St Valentine's day – a red rose or a heart – and put it on the table which members of the family are sitting round. Think about why love is important. Then begin to pass the rose or heart to each other. The person

passing it says to the person they are passing it to, 'I love you so. I love you so I will ... and then mention a way of demonstrating love (e.g. I'll give you a kiss, I'll bring you a drink next time you are thirsty, etc).The rose is taken by the person it has been given to and then they have to choose who they will give it to, and they pass it on, using their version of the same words.

When you have played this for a few minutes, perhaps you could all be still and listen as someone reads the words about love from 1 Corinthians 13. To conclude, you could pass the rose or heart around again and each mention one quality of love which you remember from the reading.

A Prayer about love

God bless all those that I love:
God bless those that love me;
God bless all those that love those that I love
and all those that love those that love me. Amen.

(From an old New England sampler.)

Pancake Day: Shrove Tuesday

Pancake Day is the day before Ash Wednesday, when Lent begins. It used to be the day when people cleared all the rich food out of their houses before the fast of Lent began. All the odds and ends that were left were mixed up together, heated up and put inside pancakes so they could be eaten up.

Be sure to have pancakes to eat today and if you hear of a pancake party happening, be sure to go to it. You might also like to have a meal made up of leftovers that are in the fridge.

Another tradition at this time in some parts of the world is carnival. You can't have a whole carnival in your house but you could all dress up in funny clothes and use face paints to make funny faces. Then eat your pancakes when you're dressed up.

Pancake Recipe

100g (4oz) flour
1 egg
250ml (10 fl oz) milk
1 tablespoon of oil
pinch of salt

Sift the flour and salt into a jug, add the egg and beat until smooth, then add the milk a drop at a time until you have a smooth liquid. When you have made the batter, it is helpful to put it all in a big jug, so that you can pour a little at a time into the frying pan to make the pancakes. Pour in just enough to cover the base of the frying pan thinly, to make crisp, thin pancakes.

Fry in oil in a flat, thick-based frying pan which is very hot.

Make sure that you make the batter together and that small children all have a turn at stirring it. Older children can try their hand at tossing pancakes. It's best to use a frying pan with a thick base and to turn the first few with a slice or knife as they are the ones most likely to stick. After that, it's easy!

Let people choose their own filling for the pancakes. Allow a free choice – this meal must be fun.

After the pancakes, decide together whether there is a way you can make Lent a special time for you this year. Look through the Lent pages of this book and find something you could do.

Say the Lord's Prayer together before bedtime.

March and April

Have a clear-out: Ash Wednesday

This is the day when Lent begins: a time of the year when we get ready for Easter by saying sorry for things we do wrong and trying especially hard to do better.

God promises that if we admit our sins and say sorry, we will always be forgiven so we can start again.

Ash Wednesday often falls in spring half-term week, and even if it doesn't you could do the following activity in the evening, or the Saturday or Sunday before.

Have a clear-out

You might find it useful to sort out the toy cupboard, a bedroom or even the shed or garage or you could find a corner that has collected all sorts of bits and pieces over several months. Sort everything out and decide what to do with it.

Then give everybody the opportunity to think about which bad habits or bad bits of themselves they would like to clear out. You could sit down together and do this – or

21

you could each go to a separate space somewhere if you prefer. Cut big paper crosses out of waste paper and give everyone a cross to hold while they think about their 'bad bits'. After about five minutes come back together again, screw up the paper crosses and put them in with the rubbish to be thrown away.

Use this prayer together:

Almighty God, our heavenly Father,
we have sinned against you,
through our own fault,
in thought and word and deed,
and in what we have left undone.
For your Son our Lord Jesus Christ's sake,
forgive us all that is past;
and grant that we may serve you in newness of life
to the glory of your name. Amen.

(from Lent, Holy Week, Easter, p. 60)

If we say we have no sin, we deceive ourselves and the truth is not in us. If we confess our sins, God is faithful and just, and will forgive us our sins and cleanse us from all unrighteousness.

1 John 1.8,9

Collect up the palm crosses

If you have palm crosses in your house kept since last year, take them out today, as Lent begins. Go round the house carefully and make sure that you have not missed any. In some churches they are burnt to make ash to use at the Ash Wednesday service.

10

A Grace Jar: something to do each day in Lent

Use an old glass jam jar with a metal top or empty tin which has a metal lid (for example a cocoa or syrup tin). Cut a slit in the lid so that coins can be put through. (This can be done with a chisel or similar tool. It must be done by a grown-up.) Make a paper label to fit the jar and label it 'The Grace Jar'. It could be decorated too. (This can be done by a child.)

Use the Grace Jar to collect money throughout Lent, which is the forty days from Ash Wednesday to Easter. (Many diaries tell you when Ash Wednesday is.) When Easter comes and the jar is full, collect up the money and send it to a charity. You could send it to Christian Aid (PO Box 100, London SE1 7RT) or find the address of your favourite charity and send it there.

Here are some ways that you could gather up the money.

Everyone puts in a small coin before each meal as a way of saying thank you for having enough to eat.

Give up something which is really a bit of a luxury for the duration of Lent:

* if you often have chocolate biscuits,
  you could have plain ones instead

* children might be able to give up sweets
  on the way home from school

* a grown up might be able to give up
  a glass of beer or wine

* drink water instead of juice at meal times

Put the money that is saved by this in the tin.

Lent is a time when we remember that Jesus went into the wilderness for forty days all alone. He was very hungry. It has been the tradition in Lent for Christian people to give something up, to help them remember what happened to Jesus and as a reminder of what it is like to be hungry and to be tempted. Today, it also helps us to remember what it is like for the many people in the world who are often hungry

because they live in places where there is not enough food, or they are too poor to buy enough to eat.

Older children and grown-ups might like to have a sponsored fast for 24 hours in Lent. Some charities do this each year, but there is nothing to stop you organizing your own and giving the money to your chosen charity. It doesn't do healthy people any harm and you certainly find out what it feels like to be hungry! Small children and people with health problems shouldn't try it though. When you tell people what you are doing they are usually very interested!

The kind of fasting I want is this: remove the chains of oppression and the yoke of injustice and let the oppressed go free. Share your food with the hungry and open your homes to the homeless poor.

Isaiah 58.6-7 (GNB)

A prayer

Help us, dear God, to live with thankful and generous hearts this day and evermore. Amen.

(from *Prayers for Children*, p. 210)

A Lenten Tree:
something else for Lent

As Lent begins, hold a family meeting and devise together forty Lenten deeds, one for each of the forty days of Lent. Some could be especially kind actions, some could be commitments to pray, or some sacrifices. Write each deed on a separate leaf-shaped piece of paper. You could make this more refined by having paper leaves in different shades of green for each member of the family, or some for adults and some for children. It is important however, that you devise and agree the set of deeds together and that they should be acceptable to everyone, even if some are specifically suited to certain people. The idea is that you should support each other in what you set out to do, rather than have a competition! If you have used fairly thin paper it may be possible to run the blade of a pair of scissors along each leaf to curl it up slightly and hide what it written inside.

When you have a complete set of leaves, put them in an old tissue box (you may like to label it 'Lent Box'). Either draw a large bare tree on a large piece of paper or card, or find a fallen branch and secure it somewhere in your house for the duration of Lent.

Each day in Lent, people take it in turns to take out a leaf, do the deed it suggests and then the leaf is stuck on the tree. (If you are using a real branch you can hang the leaves on with cotton.) As the trees break into leaf outside, your Lenten Tree will come into leaf as Easter approaches.

As the forty days of the Lenten fast do not include Sundays, you might like to think up six treats for yourselves for the six Sundays of Lent and put these in the box too, represented as flowers, which may also be stuck onto the tree. Make them out of tissue paper and plastic coated wire bag ties.

On Easter Day you can decorate your tree with yellow and gold ribbons, to celebrate the Resurrection and your completion of Lent together.

This simple but lovely Celtic prayer for protection is particularly suitable to use during Lent. Say it every day and by the end of Lent everyone will know it off by heart. (You may need to explain the meaning of 'foes confound' but you have six weeks in which to do so!)

The circle of Jesus keep you from sorrow
The circle of Jesus today and tomorrow
The circle of Jesus your foes confound
The circle of Jesus your life surround

(David Adam, *The Edge of Glory,* p. 50)

Mothering Sunday

The origin of the British Mothering Sunday seems to be that it was a day in the year, when spring had just arrived and travel was easier again, when young servants were allowed to leave the houses where they worked and walk to visit their mothers. As they went, they picked violets from the hedgerows as a simple present. Mothering Sunday has now become a big commercial venture in Britain, but it is also a favourite day for going to church. It is a tribute to the goodness within each of us, that despite the commercialism, the heart of Mothering Sunday has remained and families want to acknowledge the important part that mothers play in their lives.

If you go out for lunch, or someone else takes over the cooking for the day, it might be fun for mothers in the family to try out this quiz about Bible mothers, in their spare time. You will need a Bible with an index, or a good Children's Bible. Look up the following names and try to find out the answers to the questions:

Rebekah   Ruth   Elizabeth   Hannah   Sarah

*   Who was accused of being drunk because she wanted a baby?

*   Who laughed because she was too old to have a baby?

*   Whose husband was struck dumb?

*   Who followed her mother-in-law to Bethlehem and there became the great-grandmother of King David?

*   Who helped her favourite son to trick his father while the other son was away hunting?

A Prayer

Heavenly Father, bless all parents;
give them thankful hearts when things go well
and in the hard times give them loving kindness;
through Jesus Christ our Lord. Amen.

(from *Prayers for Children*, p. 107)

13

Holy Week: Maundy Thursday

The day before Good Friday is often called Maundy Thursday. We remember how Jesus celebrated Passover with his disciples for the last time. Passover is a time when Jewish people remember how God rescued them from slavery in Egypt. As they celebrated together, Jesus gave thanks and broke bread, then he took a cup of wine and blessed it. He told his disciples to share the bread and drink the cup to remember him. This was the Last Supper he was to eat with his disciples before he was crucified. As Christians, we believe that Jesus died on the cross to set us free from our sins and we remember what Jesus did for us each time we remember his last supper as we celebrate Holy Communion.

Make your meal special today

Eat Matzos (unleavened bread) or pitta bread from the supermarket and have wine or grape juice to drink. You could also have some kind of main course made from lamb, as Jesus and his friends would have had at the Passover.

Before you start the meal, read about Jesus' last supper in the Bible, in St Luke's Gospel, chapter 22, verses 14 to 20.

In the country where Jesus grew up, servants used to wash the feet of visitors entering a house as a sign of respect and care. Before the last supper Jesus washed his disciples' feet to show them that he was a servant. Perhaps you could all wash each other's feet and remember what Jesus did.

I, your Lord and Teacher, have just washed your feet. You, then, should wash one another's feet.

John 13.14 (GNB)

A Maundy Thursday prayer

**Help us to serve one another, Lord, with glad hearts.
Bless all those who serve us.
We think especially of . . .**
(you may like to encourage everyone to name some people that serve and help you in your local community and worldwide.)

Holy Week: Good Friday

Today we remember Jesus' arrest, trial and crucifixion and how God loved us so much that he sent his Son to die for us and give us a new relationship with God. This happens at a time of year when many people are taking a break, heading for holidays or shopping like mad for the Easter weekend ahead. It is easy to be drawn into all this busyness unless we choose to do things differently.

Have warm hot cross buns for breakfast

(You may like to make your own using the recipe below)

250g (10 oz) plain flour

50g (2 oz) sugar

25g (1 oz) yeast or 1 tbs dried yeast

1tsp each of salt and mixed spice and half tsp of cinnamon

100g (4 oz) currants

50g (2 oz) melted butter

1 egg

200mls (7 fl oz) lukewarm milk and water

Blend the yeast with the sugar and liquid.

Mix together the dry ingredients and then knead altogether with the liquid and yeast. Leave to rise for an hour and then knead again. Make into buns and put a flour and water cross on top of each. Rise again for half an hour and then bake for 20 minutes at 220°C or Gas Mark 7.

Talk about the buns before you eat them. Look at the cross and remember that Jesus died. Smell the spices (you could open a jar of mixed spice and smell that as well if you didn't make the buns) and remember how, when he had died, Jesus' friends took his body away to be buried.

You could have a quiet day or part of the day, with no music, no tapes or CDs and no TV. Then in the evening perhaps you could play some quiet music that will help you remember what a special day it is.

You could read the story of Jesus' burial in the Bible in St Luke's Gospel, chapter 23, verses 50-56.

A Good Friday Prayer

Make a little cross out of cocktail sticks for everyone to hold while you say this prayer.

> **Behold the wood of the cross on which the Saviour of the world hung and died.**
> **As we smell the sweet spices, help us to remember to be faithful like the people who buried Jesus. Amen.**

Holy Week:
Easter Eve (Holy Saturday)

Today we remember that a man called Joseph from the town of Arimathea went to Pilate and asked for the body of Jesus. Then he wrapped it in a linen cloth and laid it in a tomb carved out of the rock where no one had ever been laid. You can read this in the Bible in St Luke's Gospel, chapter 24 ,verses 52 and 53.

Make your own Easter garden

Go for a walk and find the things you need or collect them from your own garden:

∗ a few good-sized stones

∗ some moss

You will also need:

* Three crosses made out of twigs bound together with thread
* A tray or baking tin
* Some soil or sand
* Some tinfoil
* An eggcup or small vase

Line the tray or tin with foil and fill it with sand or soil. Use the stones to build the tomb. Choose a nice round stone to make the door. Make a space in the soil for an eggcup and fill it with water and flowers, or you could plant a primula or other small plant in the soil. Arrange the moss over the rest of the soil to look like grass. Make the crosses and stick them in the soil.

If you don't have access to a garden or a place to walk, use a shoebox lid and colour the inside with green paint or felt pen. Decorate it with gummed flowers. Make three crosses out of lolly sticks. Stick them upright at one end using sticky tape.

Parents might like to use the garden to talk about Good Friday and then on Saturday night, roll back the stone and sprinkle chocolate eggs in the garden, to be found on Sunday morning.

An Easter Prayer

Lord Jesus, thank you that you died for me.
Thank you for your love.
Thank you that you rose again.
Thank you for your love. Amen.

Holy Week: Easter Day

Jesus Christ is risen today! Alleluia!

Today is Easter Day, the happiest day of the year. We remember that Jesus did not stay in the tomb but came back to life, breaking for ever the power of death over us and giving us a new start with God. Try and make today really special.

 ## Remember to move the stone on the tomb of your Easter garden if you have one

Have an egg hunt before breakfast. Hide small chocolate eggs around the house or garden, depending on the weather and the temperature. Give everyone a little container so that they have somewhere safe to keep the eggs that they find. The person

who hides the eggs needs to remember how many there were so that you know when they are all found and people can stop looking.

Have a breakfast party with eggs, light a candle and have some flowers to make it special. You may like to read the story of the Resurrection as it is told in St Luke's Gospel, chapter 24, verses 1-11.

If you like presents at Easter, consider using a cardboard Easter egg for each member of the family and any guests. Fill each with a little gift (like a new pair of socks, tights or a hair band) that is inexpensive and emphasizes the truth that Easter is a time of new beginnings, new starts.

An Easter Prayer

Lord Jesus Christ
risen from the tomb,
your love fills the world.
Let it fill our hearts
so that we may follow you for ever
and show your love to everyone. Amen.

The angel spoke to the women. 'You must not be afraid,' he said. 'I know you are looking for Jesus, who was crucified. He is not here; he has been raised, just as he said. Come here and see the place where he was lying. Go quickly now and tell his disciples, "He has been raised from death, and now he is going to Galilee ahead of you; there you will see him!" Remember what I have told you.'

Matthew 28.5-7 (GNB)

Signs of new life: Eastertide

Spring is an exciting time of the year to be out and about and really helps us to explore the idea of Jesus rising from the dead.

On a warm spring day, go out and count as many signs of new life as you can. Look out for:

* the first bees buzzing round the opening flowers
* opening buds
* pussy willow
* the yellow flowers opening in the oilseed rape fields
* early butterflies

Older children may like to keep a diary of the dates that trees come into leaf: will the weeping willow beat the hawthorn, which horse chestnut will be first? You could keep a book from one year to the next, bringing it out each spring and comparing the dates on which certain plants first come into leaf, or burst into flower.

Plant a few grass seeds in a plastic pot and watch them grow. When the grass is a few centimetres high, dig down into the pot again and look at what happened to the seed. Only an empty shell is left but all that new life has come out of it.

You could let your grass seed grow in the pot and see if it will flower and develop seeds.

Read the story of *The Very Hungry Caterpillar*. Most little children enjoy this and it is available in all bookshops and libraries. The caterpillar can only become a beautiful butterfly by going into a chrysalis and waiting. It looks dead for a time but then out comes something much more beautiful than before.

Jesus said 'I am telling you the truth: a grain of wheat remains no more than a single grain unless it is dropped into the ground and dies. If it does die, then it produces many grains.'

John 12.24 (GNB)

Prayers

Write one of these prayers on a little card and illustrate
it with pictures of new life.

**Living Lord Jesus, help us see that
You are Lord.**

(Patrick Appleford)

**Rejoice, O earth, in shining splendour,
radiant in the brightness of your King!
Christ has conquered! Glory fills you!
Darkness vanishes for ever!**

(Exsultet, the Easter Song of Praise, from *Lent, Holy Week, Easter*, p. 230)

Go on a lamb hunt: Eastertide

 If you are able to get out into the countryside, it is fun to go on a lamb hunt. And even if you can't reach the country, you may be able to find a city farm with some lambs.

Spend some time watching the lambs running and playing. You could decide which is the funniest lamb, or the most daring or the cutest. You might try giving some of them names.

At home you could make a shepherd's crook by rolling newspaper tightly into a long roll and bending over the top, and use a toy lamb to play at being a shepherd.

Find the story which Jesus told about the lost sheep. You might find it in a Children's Bible or you can find it in St Matthew's Gospel, chapter 18, verses 12 to 14. There are lots of little Bible story books which tell this story too.

I am the good shepherd, who is willing to die for the sheep.

John 10.11 (GNB)

A Prayer

Lord Jesus, the Good Shepherd,
You look after those who have strayed and are lost;

Look after our lives so that we become your friends
and stay close to you today and forever. Amen.

(from *Prayers for Children*, p. 200)

If you can't get out into the countryside to see sheep and lambs, perhaps you could find out if there is anyone who has a cat which has recently had kittens or a dog with puppies, or maybe even a rabbit with babies, and you could watch these baby animals for a bit, then talk about the new life of spring.

Crop spotting: Rogationtide

The word Rogation comes from '*rogare*', the Latin word for 'to ask'. When we see on the TV people who have not been able to grow their food because of war or bad weather, we remember how lucky we are to have food. Farmers are always aware of how easy it would be for everything to go wrong and for nothing to grow at all. Sometimes it's too dry and sometimes it's too wet. So at the very end of Eastertide, on the three days before Ascension Day, when we can see the fields green with new life, farmers traditionally prayed for their crops.

Discover what it's like to grow your own food

Small children will enjoy growing something to eat themselves. It is fascinating to watch something turn from a seed to a little shoot to something you can eat. Radishes or lettuces grow fairly quickly and you can buy the seeds in supermarkets. Use a large pot, even if you have a garden, so your crop is not eaten by something else before you! You will need to care for it and watch it every day.

Or go on a crop spotting walk

Older children and grown-ups may enjoy a crop spotting walk. Use a map to find a route which takes you around lots of fields and see if you can identify what you see growing.

You show your care for the land by sending rain;
you make it rich and fertile.
You fill the streams with water;
you provide the earth with crops. . . .

You send abundant rain on the ploughed fields and soak them with water;

you soften the soil with showers and cause the young plants to grow.

from Psalm 65 (GNB)

A Prayer

Each time you look at your pot of growing food,
you could say this prayer:

We praise you, O God, and we bless you,
for you give us food from the earth. Amen.

May and June

Little things: Mother Julian of Norwich, 8 May

Little children, and other people, love small things. We may love kittens or hamsters. Or we may collect little stones or shells. Some people collect tiny toys. And sometimes we pick up little seeds or nuts from the trees. Sometimes we play with beautiful beads or buttons or look at a handful of sand and see all the different tiny grains.

Mother Julian lived a life dedicated to God all on her own in Norwich six hundred years ago. Her tiny house was built into the wall of a church and had three windows. One looked into the church; one looked onto the road (so people could come and ask her advice) and one let in the light. At one point in her life, Mother Julian was very ill, and she became very aware of God's love. Later she wrote down what she had learnt. One of her visions was of a little thing:

'God showed me a little thing, no bigger than a hazelnut, lying in the palm of my hand...In this little thing I saw three truths: the first is that God made it, the second is that God loves it, the third is that God keeps it...In truth, I saw the Creator, the Lover and the Keeper.'

Find some small things to look at today and let each person hold something in the palm of their hand. Look at each little thing carefully: touch it and feel it. Describe it and say what is wonderful about it. Then say the words of Mother Julian:

'God showed me a little thing... lying in the palm of my hand. In this little thing I saw three truths: the first is that God made it, the second is that God loves it, the third is that God keeps it.'

Perhaps you might like to remember Mother Julian's words from time to time. You might make a collection of little things at different times of the year and lay them out carefully in a corner or on a tray for a while. Light a candle beside them and write Mother Julian's words on a card to go beside them.

Perhaps someone might like to draw a picture of Mother Julian in her tiny house with its three windows beside the church.

Make up a prayer

Thank God for little things and for his care for you.

Christian Aid Week: May

Christian Aid Week is always in the second or third week of May. During this time Christians all over Britain make a special effort to raise money to help people in the poor countries of the world. With the money raised, Christian Aid works in partnership with 700 different local organisations in 60 different countries. Another important part of its work is the campaigns that it runs in Britain to make people more aware of the need to work fairly to help the world's poorest people.

I was hungry and you fed me, thirsty and you gave me a drink; I was a stranger and you received me in your homes, naked and you clothed me; I was sick and you took care of me, in prison and you visited me.

Matthew 25.35-36 (GNB)

You can read what Jesus said about caring for the poor in the Bible. Read St Matthew's Gospel, chapter 25, verses 31 to 46.

There are lots of ways in which families can help with Christian Aid Week. Find out what the church in your neighbourhood is doing during Christian Aid Week and offer to help.

Children can't collect money on their own, but they can help to deliver envelopes from door to door and they can help grown-ups to collect money. Even someone in a buggy can carry the bag of envelopes – and this is a chance to meet new faces.

Go to the church and look at the Christian Aid posters. Find out about some of the pictures you see there.

Older children may like to find out if there are any children's events for Christian Aid Week and ask at school if there is going to be a special Christian Aid Week assembly.

If you like to surf the web, you can find out up to date information about Christian Aid at www.christian-aid.org.uk

A Prayer

Here is a special prayer to say every day during Christian Aid Week.

May our hands be your hands, O God,
gathering in the harvest.
May our feet be your feet,
bringing good news for the poor.
May our hearts be full of compassion,
inviting all whom we meet
to open their heart too,
in the name of Jesus Christ. Amen.

(Christian Aid)

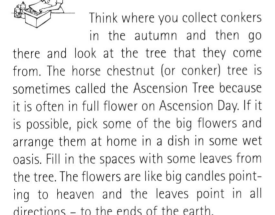

Ascension

For forty days after he rose from the dead, Jesus kept appearing to his friends. He promised to send the Holy Spirit to help them take his message to the ends of the earth. Then he left them. So Ascension Day is always on a Thursday, exactly forty days after Easter.

Think where you collect conkers in the autumn and then go there and look at the tree that they come from. The horse chestnut (or conker) tree is sometimes called the Ascension Tree because it is often in full flower on Ascension Day. If it is possible, pick some of the big flowers and arrange them at home in a dish in some wet oasis. Fill in the spaces with some leaves from the tree. The flowers are like big candles pointing to heaven and the leaves point in all directions – to the ends of the earth.

The apostles still had their eyes fixed on the sky as he went away, when two men dressed in white suddenly stood beside them and said 'Galileans, why are you standing there looking up at the sky? This Jesus, who was taken away from you into heaven will come back in the same way that you saw him go into heaven.'

Acts 1.10-11 (GNB)

You can find the whole story in the Bible in Acts, chapter 1.

Jesus said 'And I will be with you always, to the end of the age.'

Matthew 28.20 (GNB)

It is still the tradition in some places to try and go to a high place on Ascension Day. At Magdalen College in Oxford the choir go to the top of the chapel tower and sing a hymn. People from the city go to the bottom of the tower to listen.

Perhaps if you have time, you could go to a high place too. If there is a hill near to where you live, you might like to go up it. Or maybe you could organize to go to the top of your church tower. There will be a wonderful view from the top. But if there are going to be quite a few children, make sure you have enough grown-ups to supervise them.

A Prayer

Lord God,
you are the King of the Universe,
King of Creation,
and King of Glory.
We worship you on this kingly day. Amen.

(from *Prayers for Children*, p. 230)

Pentecost

Pentecost is a Greek word meaning 'the fiftieth day'. Pentecost is the fiftieth day after the Jewish Passover and is the day when the Holy Spirit came to Jesus' disciples. They felt the Spirit as wind and tongues of flame.

Celebrate Pentecost in your home

It is a Jewish tradition to celebrate Pentecost by decorating the home with flowers and greenery. Decorate your house by going out to gather some flowers and greenery to make into a flower arrangement together. If you used only red and white flowers, they would help to remind you of the wind and flames. Put lots of candles either into or around the flowers: they could be red and white too. Light them when you are all together, perhaps for a meal.

Go kite flying

If it's a windy day, you could go out and fly a kite somewhere. Enjoy the wind in your hair and on your faces.

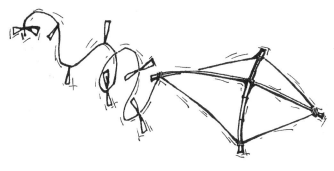

I will pour out my Spirit on everyone;
your sons and daughters will proclaim my message;
your old people will have dreams,
and your young people will see visions.
At that time I will pour out my Spirit even on servants,
both men and women.

Joel 2.28-29 (GNB)

Read the Story of Pentecost in the Bible in Acts, chapter 2, or find it in a Children's Bible.

A Prayer: Tongues of Fire

Fire is red and burning and very powerful . . .
O God, warm our heart and our lives
that we may radiate your love to the world for
Jesus sake. Amen.

(from *Prayers for Children*, p. 231)

Trinity Sunday

On the Sunday after Pentecost, we celebrate the Trinity. Trinity means three and this is when Christians focus on God as Father, Son and Holy Spirit: three and yet one. It is impossible fully to explain the Trinity but we know God as Father, (the Creator who made us), Son (who came to earth for us in Jesus) and Holy Spirit (who is at work in our lives).

Anything we can do to understand this is only a picture of something far more wonderful, but perhaps we can begin to have a glimmer of what it means by doing this experiment.

You will need:

* a large bowl of water
* a jug
* an ice tray from the freezer
* a kettle
* children and adults working together

Dip the jug into the water, pour the water into the ice tray and put it into the freezer for a while.

When the water is frozen, dip the jug into the bowl of water again and pour the water into the kettle.

Boil the kettle and watch the steam, get the ice out of the freezer and have look at it. Look at and talk about the water, the ice and the steam.

Something else to do

Think of as many words beginning with tri- or tre as you can. Children who are at school will know that tri- indicates three. If you have time you could perhaps spend some time making a little collection of three-sided or three-leaved items.

A Trinity Prayer

Thank you Lord that you are Father,
Son and Holy Spirit.
Help us to know you better and to love you more. Amen.

Corpus Christi: the Thursday after Trinity Sunday

Corpus Christi means 'The Body of Christ'. For centuries, some churches have used the Thursday after Trinity Sunday to say a special thank you for Holy Communion. If there are children in your family who receive Holy Communion already, or who will before long, you might like to set aside some time to think about it especially at this time. Use a basket of bread as a focus.

Provide some bread

You could bake a loaf yourselves. Or you could go to the shop and let everyone choose the kind of bread they particularly like and then put a portion for each person in a basket in the middle of the table. Sit around the table, set nicely with a clean cloth, some flowers or a plant and a candle. Invite everyone to take a piece of bread from the basket and hold it while you say this prayer together or one person says it for everyone:

Blessed are You, Lord our God, king of the universe, who brings forth food out of the earth.

Read some stories from the New Testament about Jesus breaking bread with his friends. It might be good, if it is possible, for each person present to read one short story. You could use a Children's Bible for some of the stories:

Jesus breaks bread with two people on the road to Emmaus: Luke 24.13-16, 28-32
Jesus shares his last supper with his disciples: Luke 22.14-20
Jesus tells the crowd that he is the bread of life: John 6.35-40
The risen Jesus meets the disciples after a fishing trip: John 21.1-13

Talk together about what you each imagine it must have been like for one person in some of the stories. People can choose but if you need an idea to start you off, think what it might have been like for Peter at the last supper, or for one of the people who was with Jesus on the road to Emmaus, or one of the disciples at the end of the fishing trip.

Talk about being at a service of Holy Communion. What feels particularly special about it? What do you notice each time?

A Prayer

Remind yourselves that when you receive Holy Communion you are remembering that Jesus died for your sins and rose again to assure you of new life, and he did that for each of us because we are precious to him and not because we deserve it. To help you remember this, someone could read this prayer which is sometimes used at Communion services:

Most merciful Lord,
your love compels us to come in.
Our hands were unclean,
our hearts were unprepared;
we were not fit
even to eat the crumbs from under your table.
But you, Lord, are the God of our salvation,
and share your bread with sinners.
So cleanse and feed us
with the precious body and blood of your Son,
that he may live in us and we in him;
and that we, with the whole company of Christ,
may sit and eat in your kingdom. Amen.

(from *Common Worship*)

John the Baptist: 24 June

June 24 is the birthday of John the Baptist. John was born three months after the Annunciation, when we remember how Mary was told by an angel that she was to be the mother of Jesus. We remember the Annunciation on 25 March, exactly nine months before Christmas Day. This is why St John the Baptist's day is 24 June. You can find the story in the first chapter of Luke's Gospel, verses 2 to 25.

John was called the Baptist because he prepared people to hear Jesus, calling them to stop doing things they shouldn't do and to be baptized in the River Jordan.

Think about being sorry and do something about it:

* THINK of something you have done or said
  which you wish you hadn't
* TAKE a washable felt pen, a bowl of water,
  soap and a flannel or nailbrush
* WRITE or DRAW what you would like to say sorry
  for, on your hand.
* WASH it off

A Prayer

Thank you Lord that when we are sorry, you forgive us and wash away the wrong things we have done. Amen.

When he was a man, John often went into the desert and when he was there, one of the things he ate was wild honey. Try and have honey for breakfast or tea today to remind you of John the Baptist.

John went throughout the whole territory of the River Jordan, preaching, 'Turn away from your sins and be baptized, and God will forgive your sins.'

Luke 3.3 (GNB)

27

St Peter's Day: 29 June

On 29 June we remember Peter the fisherman, who was one of Jesus' best friends. His first name was Simon, but Jesus gave him a new name, Peter, which means 'a rock'. Peter was one of the first followers and seems to have been very close to Jesus. In St Matthew's Gospel we are told that Jesus said to him 'I will give you the keys of the Kingdom of heaven'. If you see old pictures or carvings of Jesus' disciples, you can nearly always pick out Peter immediately because he is shown carrying a key. Try looking for him if you visit old churches. You will be surprised how often you can spot him.

 ## Have fish to eat today

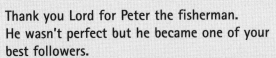

A Prayer

You could say this prayer before your fish meal.

> **Thank you Lord for Peter the fisherman.**
> **He wasn't perfect but he became one of your**
> **best followers.**
> **Help us to know your forgiveness when we do silly things**
> **and make us good followers too. Amen.**

There are lots of stories about Peter in the Bible. Find out how he left his job as a fisherman to follow Jesus in St Luke's Gospel, chapter 5. And find out how he really let Jesus down (in St Matthew's Gospel, chapter 26) yet was still one of the first people to find the empty tomb on Easter morning (in St John's Gospel, chapter 20).

You can make simple paper weights to remind you of St Peter. Find a stone (a small rock!) with one flat, smooth side. Wash and dry it if it is dirty. Put a key on the flat smooth side and draw round it with an indelible felt pen. Remove the real key and colour in the outline. To preserve your handiwork, varnish it, so that the ink is not rubbed off. Clear nail varnish will do this in a simple way. You could add other pictures to your rock: fish or boats perhaps. If you know someone called Peter, you may like to give him the rock. You could paint one for a different Peter each year!

July and August

A water day: July

Plan a day in the holidays for playing with water. You could go swimming or go out on a boat. You may like to do some fishing, however simple, or play beside a stream. Perhaps you could have a picnic beside the river or visit a waterfall. You might even be able to visit an aquarium or water theme park. Little people might like to have a paddling pool out or play with water toys. If it's very hot, have a water fight.

You could also make bubble pictures. Add some paint to a mixture of water and detergent and then blow lots of big bubbles into the water using straws. Lay paper across the bubbles and see what sort of picture you get.

You could also allow people to choose their own drinks today and talk together about what you are doing as you make them. Talk about what it feels like to be very thirsty.

Then visit a church and look at the font, the place where people are baptized. You may have to make special arrangements to get in, if the church is kept locked, but no one will mind if you ask. Go and stand around the font and think about why being christened is so special. Why is water important when people are baptized? What does it remind us of?

If you are at a church where any of the children were baptized, someone might be able to show you the baptism book with their names in it.

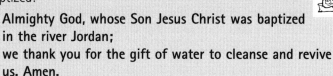

A Prayer

This is part of a prayer used for blessing the water when people are baptized:

Almighty God, whose Son Jesus Christ was baptized in the river Jordan;
we thank you for the gift of water to cleanse and revive us. Amen.

(from *Common Worship*)

If some people know the song '*The water of life*' they may like to teach it to everyone else.

Shell collecting:
St James' Day, 25 July

If you go to the beach, spend some time collecting shells. See how many different whole shells you can collect. You might like to take a shell book and see if you can work out what used to live in the shells. If the tide is out for long enough and you are on a sandy beach, you could use the shells to make a picture in the sand. Or you could take all your shells home and make them into a little museum for a day or two as a reminder of your trip. Lay them out carefully on some blue paper or cloth.

Shells remind us of St James. He was a fisherman who went to be one of Jesus' disciples and was with Jesus for three years. You can read his story in St Matthew's Gospel, chapter 8 or you might like to find it in a Children's Bible.

Spanish people are especially fond of St James and people used to travel from all over Europe to visit the Cathedral at Santiago de Compostela in western Spain where he is particularly remembered. In pictures he is often shown as a pilgrim wearing a cloak, with a hat to keep off the sun, a gourd full of wine, a stick to help him along and a scallop shell to remind him of being a fisherman, called by Jesus. Perhaps you could draw a picture of him and colour it in.

A special St James prayer

Dear God, help us to remember how
James left everything he had to follow Jesus:
help us to be ready to do whatever needs to be done.
Amen.

30

A holiday collage: July or August

Our word 'holiday' comes from 'holy day', a day set aside from work to thank God and to rest. During the summertime, when playgroups and schools are on holiday, why not make a collage to celebrate God's creation and say thank you for all the good things he gives us?

For the collage:

* Choose a space and outline it: if you are on a beach or in another open space, this could be quite large; if you are inside, you could use a tray with some soil or sand in.

* Collect items to make patterns: stones, seaweed, shells, drift wood, feathers, flowers such as daisies, twigs, leaves and seeds (make sure they're not poisonous).

    ✱   Divide your space up into smaller areas.

    ✱   Fill each smaller space with a collection of items that are the
                same.

If you are on a beach, you could decorate some of the spaces with patterns in the sand made with sticks to enrich the effect of different colours and textures. Perhaps you could take a photograph when your collage is finished.

A Prayer

You could leave these words beside your collage:

To see the World in a Grain of Sand
and Heaven in a Wild Flower,
hold Infinity in the palm of your hand
and Eternity in an hour.

William Blake
(from *Prayers for Children*, p. 174)

By the seventh day God finished what he had been doing and stopped working. He blessed the seventh day and set it apart as a special day, because by that day he had completed his creation and stopped working.

Genesis 2.2-3 (GNB)

31

Zacchaeus: July or August

This is a good activity for a day out in the woods and would be much more fun with two or three families. Take a picnic and wear old clothes. You might like to take a tree book and see how many different kinds of tree you can identify.

When you have finished your picnic, play hide-and-seek. The game can be as simple or elaborate as you like to make it, depending on the ages of the people involved. You could even play stalking or sardines: both would be fun. The only thing to be careful about is that no one gets lost or frightened.

When you are all tired out, find a place to sit down. If there is a suitable tree and you have tree climbers among you, they might like to climb a little way up the tree. Then listen to this story.

When Jesus visited the town of Jericho, Zacchaeus the tax collector wanted to see him but because he was a very small man, he couldn't see over the crowd. So he climbed a tree to get a better view. When Jesus came past he saw Zacchaeus up in the tree and told him to come down. 'I want to stay with you tonight', he said. Everyone else began to complain. They didn't like Zacchaeus because he had become very rich by cheating them. But Zacchaeus welcomed Jesus and was changed by meeting him. 'I will give away half of all I have', he said, 'and I will pay back the people I have cheated'. Jesus said 'Welcome back. I came to look for lost people and save them'.

A Prayer

Thank you Lord, that you welcome us.
Help us to be honest.
Help us to be kind and generous,
and always on the lookout for people who need help.
Amen.

Before you go home you could pick up some leaves and twigs from the floor of your wood to make a wood collage when you get home. Then you could make a little figure of Zacchaeus and hide him in one of your trees.

32

A journey game: July or August

Here is a game you might like to play for a bit with older children if you are on a journey in the car or on a bus or train. There are no right or wrong answers but the ideas are lots of fun.

Take it in turns to talk about ways to think of God – like this:

'I think that if God were an animal,
God would be a whale because God is bigger than anything we can imagine'
or
'God would be a dog, because he keeps us safe'

'If God were a musical instrument,
God would be a triangle, because you can hear God's voice above everything else, but it isn't loud . . '.

'If God were the weather . . '.
'If God were a piece of furniture . . '.
'If God were a flower . . '.
'If God were a colour . . '.

How many other things can you think of?

One of the best Bible stories about a journey describes two of Jesus disciples travelling along a road after the crucifixion. They are very sad that Jesus has died. Suddenly they are joined by a stranger who explains all sorts of things to them. When they reach the house he goes in with them and breaks bread. Then they recognize him – Jesus, risen from the dead!

You can read the whole story in St Luke's Gospel, chapter 24, starting at verse 13.

A Prayer

Dear God
We cannot really imagine what you are like.
You are a mystery.
But sometimes we just catch glimpses
which help us to understand things a bit.
Thank you for being there. Amen.

'Wasn't it like a fire burning in us when he talked to us on the road and explained the Scriptures to us?'

Luke 24.32 (GNB)

Loaves and fishes:
July or August

This might make a supermarket trip a bit more interesting in the holidays and give you something to look forward to at the end of it. Or you could use it as a way to explore a fish market.

Find the bread section of a supermarket and choose all kinds of different bread: see if you can get some from different parts of the world. Older children might be given a basket to put it in and be left to make their own choices while grown-ups fill the trolley with other things.

Look at the different kinds of fish available. Of the smaller types buy several sorts (e.g. sprats, herrings, plaice, trout, prawns.)

At home, you might like to look on a map for the countries that the different kinds of bread come from. Have a barbecue with the fish and the bread: you could invite some friends round. Much fish is best barbecued in aluminium foil. Put the bread and fish on a big plate and eat them together as a big picnic. If fresh fish is too complicated, you could use fish fingers.

 After you have eaten, read the story of the loaves and the fishes told in the Bible in St John's Gospel chapter 6, verses 1 to 13. You can find this story in every Gospel but the important thing about the way John tells it is that the person who provides the bread and fish to feed all the people is a little boy. He hadn't got very much but he offered to share it. A little person might not have seemed very important, but without his willingness to share, the other people would not have been fed.

Try to think of people who may not seem to be very important but without whom really essential things don't happen. The grown-ups could tell the children of all the things they appreciate about them.

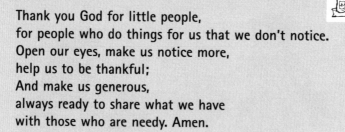

A Prayer

When you have finished talking, say a prayer for each other:

> **Thank you God for little people,**
> **for people who do things for us that we don't notice.**
> **Open our eyes, make us notice more,**
> **help us to be thankful;**
> **And make us generous,**
> **always ready to share what we have**
> **with those who are needy. Amen.**

 Can you think of a way of helping some people in need from a place where they eat one of the kinds of bread that you bought?

Ichthus – the sign of the fish:
July or August

There have been times when it has been very dangerous to be a Christian. There are even places in the world today where Christians cannot worship in safety and where their lives are made dangerous and difficult. Things were difficult like this for the first Christians and many of them survived by hiding. So they needed secret signs so that Christian people would recognize one another and not be afraid. One of these secret signs was a fish.

The reason that the fish was chosen as a secret sign is that the Greek word for fish is ICHTHUS and the letters which spell the word are the first letters of the Greek words for Jesus Christ, Son of God, Saviour

Jesus	Iesus
Christ	Christos
of God	Theou
Son	Uios
Saviour	Soter

Christians in danger

We can read in the Bible, in Acts chapter 12, verses 1 to 6, about two Christians in danger. James and Peter were sent to prison. If you want to find out about how Peter made an amazing escape, you could read on.

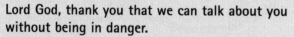 You could find out about Christians in danger today and perhaps write a letter or send a card to let them know they have a friend. To find out about this, write to Christian Solidarity at PO Box 99, Dept 97/5 New Malden, Surrey, KT3 3YF.

Some people still wear the fish sign today. You see stickers on car windows and some people wear a little gold badge. You could make your own fish badge very simply by using an ordinary bought round card badge and decorating it with a really pretty fish. Wear it for a week and see if anyone asks you about it.

A Prayer

Pray for Christians who cannot worship freely today:

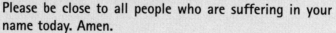

Lord God, thank you that we can talk about you without being in danger.
Please be close to all people who are suffering in your name today. Amen.

35

St Aidan: 31 August

Aidan was an Irishman but spent a large part of his life walking around the north of England telling people about Jesus and so we remember him as a missionary. Aidan lived in the seventh century and was a great friend of the King of Northumbria, Oswald. He was made a bishop and lived in a monastery on Holy Island or Lindisfarne, an island off the coast of north-east England which can be reached on foot over a causeway when the tide is out. From here he walked all over the place teaching people and showing them how to live through the example of his own good life.

Go for a walk

Make 31 August a day to go for a walk and remember St Aidan. The summer holidays are drawing to an end and the evenings are now getting shorter so make the best of the time that is left to enjoy a bit of space. As you walk, talk a bit about what you would have told people about Jesus if you had been St Aidan. What is important about Jesus to you? Sometimes when you have thought about these things together, it's easier to answer questions people might ask you one day when you are not expecting it! If you like singing as you walk, you could sing the song *'I the Lord of sea and sky'*, which can remind us that Aidan went out across the sea and under the wild skies, being God's messenger to people who needed to hear of God's love. It also reminds us that God calls each of us to be his messengers too.

Draw St Aidan and visit Lindisfarne

You might like to try and visit Lindisfarne one day, if you are ever in the north-east of England. Walking across the causeway at low tide is very exciting and you will certainly still find that it is a Holy Island and a place where people pray and feel close to God. People who like drawing might like to create a picture of St Aidan walking out on his own across the wild northern hills.

A Prayer for St Aidan's Day

Send me Lord.
I will go, Lord, if you lead me:
I will hold your people in my heart.

(From the song *'I the Lord of sea and sky'*)

I heard the Lord say, 'Whom shall I send? Who will be our messenger?' I answered, 'I will go! Send me!'

Isaiah 6.8 (GNB)

78

September and October

36

Holy Cross Day:
14 September

The cross is Christianity's most important symbol, reminding us all of Jesus' death and resurrection.

We are signed with the cross when we are baptized, to show that we have been baptized into Jesus' death and resurrection. The cross is like a special badge, showing that we belong to Jesus. Some people wear a cross round their necks to remind them of this and to show people they meet that they are a Christian. Some people wear a little cross badge in their coat and sometimes people have a cross on the wall in their house. If you look around you may be able to spot crosses outside too.

Count the crosses today

Try and keep a count of how many crosses you see today, both inside and outside. At the end of the day you might like to see who found the largest number. The person who found the most may like to tell everyone where they saw them and if they went anywhere special!

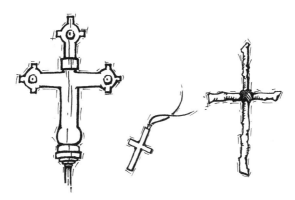

If you do not have one already, you might like to make a cross for your home or bedroom. A very simple one could be made from twigs, bound together with thread. It is important to remember that the cross upon which Jesus died would have been rough and cruel, knocked together for the purpose, so you should not be ashamed of a simple cross. If you want to make something more special, or a cross to wear, you could use some kind of modelling medium which dries or may be baked and can be painted and glazed. Don't forget to make a hole in the top to hang it by. If you were given a cross as a present at your baptism, but don't often wear it, today would be a good day to get it out. Say the prayer below when you put on the cross.

A Prayer

Here is a special prayer about the cross which has been used by Christians for many centuries. People often say it when they first go into a church and kneel down to pray. It is very short and easy to learn.

> **We adore you, O Christ, and we bless you,**
> **Because by your holy cross you have redeemed the world.**
> **Amen.**

A good book to read today would be *The Tale of Three Trees* by Angela Elwell Hunt. It is published by Lion.

37

Money, money, money:
St Matthew's Day, 21 September

September 21 is St Matthew's Day. Matthew was a tax collector, and therefore probably quite rich but very unpopular, when Jesus called him to be one of his followers. You can read the story in St Matthew's Gospel, chapter 9.

You could use St Matthew's Day or some time round about it, to make family plans for the way in which you give your money. As Christians we believe that God the Creator gives us all that we have and, in response to this generosity, we must make serious decisions about the way we give a proportion of our time and money to do God's work in the world. Doing this as a family is challenging, but important, for we can all learn from each other by talking about what we do and believe. What we don't talk about may remain hidden.

Here are some ideas to think about:

Are there ways to plan the way you give money, if you have a regular income? (Envelopes at the church, standing orders at the bank, a charity money box into which everyone puts a proportion of their wages or pocket money or a Charities Aid Foundation account.)

* Decide which you think are really important charities.

* Could you set aside a sum in order to respond to a disaster fund when there is a crisis?

* How do you give time to help others or raise money for them?

* Could you join a campaign which works for justice for poor and oppressed people?

A good craft activity today might be coin rubbing. Take a coin and put a sheet of paper over it. Rub it carefully with a wax crayon until you have the pattern of the coin on the paper. You could try patterns from coins from other countries too if you have them, for a bit of extra interest.

A Prayer

This is the special prayer for St Matthew's Day.

Almighty God,
who through your Son Jesus Christ
called Matthew from the selfish pursuit of gain
to become an apostle and evangelist:
free us from all possessiveness and love of riches
that we may follow in the steps of Jesus Christ our Lord.
Amen.

38

St Michael and All Angels: 29 September

On 29 September we remember the angels. Some of the last flowers of summer, long-stemmed purple asters with a yellow centre, are called Michaelmas daisies after one of the angels in the Bible who is given a name, Michael. (You can find out about it in the Old Testament, in the Book of Daniel chapter 10.)

Make an angel corner in your house for a few days

Go out and find some Michaelmas daisies. Pick a bunch and put it in a vase. Make an angel chain by tracing the template onto the folded edge of a concertina of paper and then cutting it out. Decorate your angels with gold and silver pens and glitter, to look very beautiful. Put them with the Michaelmas daisies in a corner of the house somewhere and leave them there for a week.

Copy out these words from Psalm 91 (verses 11 and 12) and put them beside the flowers and the angels, or leave a Bible open at Psalm 91.

God will put his angels in charge of you
to protect you wherever you go.
They will hold you up with their hands
to keep you from hurting your feet on the stones.

(GNB)

More about angels

In the Bible angels are often messengers, like the angel Gabriel who announced to Mary that she would have a son, or the angels who told the shepherds of the birth of Jesus. Sometimes they fulfil the role of protectors who care for people, like the angels who came and ministered to Jesus after he had been tempted in the wilderness.

The idea of someone being there for us, to represent God's care, is very powerful and comforting. Meister Eckhart, an old German teacher, said simply, 'That's all an angel is, an idea of God.'

A very old prayer for God's care

Keep watch, dear Lord,
with those who work,
or watch, or weep this night
and give your angels care over those who sleep.
Tend the sick, Lord Christ;
give rest to the weary,
bless the dying, soothe the suffering,
pity the afflicted, shield the joyous
and all for your love's sake. Amen.

(from *The Office of Compline*)

39

St Francis:
4 October

Francis has always been one of the best loved saints and there are many, many stories about him. He was a rich young man who became very ill and as a result of this decided to devote his life to working with the poor. He spent much of his time caring for people with leprosy who were outcasts because of their illness, and with beggars. But he still found time to rebuild a ruined church and to praise God all the time.

A family St Francis project

Stories about St Francis are not hard to find. A family with older children might like to spend some time finding as many as possible from books at home, at church, at school, in the library, and from information on the Internet. Then use the stories you have found to write your own little life of St Francis in a picture-word format for younger children. It could begin like this.

Francis was born into a rich . . . He became a . . . and was . . .

Here are some clue words:

Assisi   Rome   poor   creation

battle   clothes   ruined   companions

crucifix

moon   praise   wolf   animals   friars

water   peace   Clare   sun   San Damiano

A Prayer

Many people love the prayer that is attributed to St Francis:

Lord, make me an instrument of your peace;
where there is hatred, let me sow love;
where there is injury, pardon;
where there is discord, union;
where there is doubt, faith;
where there is despair, hope;
where there is darkness, light;
where there is sadness, joy;
for your mercy and for your truth's sake. Amen.

40

St Luke's Day: 18 October

Luke wrote two books in the Bible, St Luke's Gospel and the Acts of the Apostles. He was a doctor, who travelled with St Paul on several of his journeys. Luke tells us that his purpose in writing his Gospel was to give his friend, Theophilus, a clear and accurate account of who Jesus was and what he taught. Luke is the patron saint of doctors and artists.

Praying for sick people

In Luke's Gospel there are lots of descriptions of sick people being healed by Jesus. You can read about a man with leprosy in chapter 5, verses 12 to 14 and about a group of people who brought their poorly friend to Jesus in chapter 4 verse 40.

Christians pray for sick people, believing God wants to heal the whole person, body, mind and spirit.

Make a prayer board

Use a big piece of cardboard or a large cereal box and divide it into two halves, one for asking prayers and one for thank-you prayers. Write the name of a sick person on a post-it note and stick it on the asking side. When you see God at work in the lives of those you have prayed for, write a thank-you prayer on a post-it note and stick it on the thank-you side of the board. You might like to decorate the other side of the box with a painting of St Luke.

Talk together about times when you were ill and what it was like.

*   What made you feel better? Did it help to know someone was praying for you?
*   Talk about people you know who are sick and how their illness affects their life.

Prayers

Pray for the people you have been talking about. With small children, use clapping hands and stamping feet:

God loves us *(clap in rhythm)*
God cares for us *(stamp in rhythm)*
God is with us now *(clap in rhythm)*

Send a card today to someone who is poorly or feeling down.

One World Week

One World Week happens towards the end of October and is an opportunity to remember that human beings throughout the world are sisters and brothers and that, however unlikely it may seem, we are all dependent on each other.

 At the beginning of the week, put a globe or a map of the world in a place where you will notice it all week. If you haven't got one, you could make your own globe, by drawing on a melon or a grapefruit.

Each day this week check the labels on all the food you eat to see where it comes from. For each item that comes from outside Britain, put a little sticker on your globe or map (e.g. a little piece of paper attached with blue tac or a sticky dot). By the end of the week, it should be well decorated.

A Prayer

As you put each sticker on your globe, remember the farmers who produced the food, especially those in countries where people are very poor, and say this short prayer:

**Loving God,
thank you for the farmers who grew this food.
Make us aware of their needs,
and hungry and thirsty for justice
for all people in the world. Amen.**

*Lord, I know that you defend the cause of the poor
and the rights of the needy.
The righteous will praise you indeed;
they will live in your presence.*

Psalm 140.12-13 (GNB)

You could find out more about One World Week and about fairly traded food by contacting Christian Aid: 020 7523 2248 or www.christian-aid.org.uk.

All Hallows Eve: 31 October

The clocks change at about this time and the evenings are dark. From ancient times European people have felt it important to mark this turn in the year as winter begins. Christians use this time to remember all the saints, who have shone like lights in dark places. We suggest carving a pumpkin with Christian symbols and letting it shine outside, as a way of showing that we are reclaiming this important time for Christ.

Here are some things to do to help you enjoy the fun of going out on a dark evening and to remember the saints who shone as lights.

Make a pumpkin lantern with Christian symbols on it

Carve a cross in one place, a dove in another, a fish in another and a cloverleaf shape (to remind people of God the Father, Son and Holy Spirit) in another. Then put a candle inside and put the lantern outside where you and everyone else can see it shining out through the little shapes into the darkness.

Find out if there was a saint who had your name (many of us are actually called after saints). Cut a piece of dark paper to the right size to wrap around a jam jar. Write your saint's name on this in big fat letters and then cut out the letters, leaving letter-shaped holes in the paper. Wrap the paper round the outside of the jam jar and stick it with tape, make a handle for the jar by wrapping some string round the rim and attaching a loop to it and put a nightlight inside the jar. Light the candle and take the jar out to a dark place where the name of the saint can shine out into the darkness. Make sure a grown-up supervises this activity - the jar gets very hot. Don't forget to bring it in the next day before the glass gets broken.

With what's left of the pumpkin, make some soup:

Roast the pumpkin flesh in a hot oven until it starts to soften. Fry an onion and some garlic in oil and when it is just soft, add the roasted pumpkin flesh chopped up roughly. Cover this with a mixture of $2/3$ water and $1/3$ milk and add salt, pepper and nutmeg. Simmer gently until the onion and pumpkin are completely soft, cool a little and then liquidize in a food processor. Serve steaming hot in bowls with a spoonful of sour cream in the middle.

A Prayer for lighting a candle

This prayer begins with an old proverb

It's better to light a candle
than to curse the darkness,
so Lord,
help us to be creators of light and slayers of darkness
in all that we do. Amen.

(from *Prayers for Children*, p. 237)

November and December

All Souls Day: 2 November

On the day after All Saints Day we have an opportunity to remember everyone who has died.

Today would be a good day to get out and explore old family photograph albums and other old treasures that have been passed down through the family. Parents may be able to remember and talk about stories about their own grandparents. What did they like doing? What was special about them?

Have you got any ancestors who did famous (or infamous) things?

You may like to try constructing your own family tree. You could do it either on paper, or by using a little branch and tying pictures of earlier family members on it.

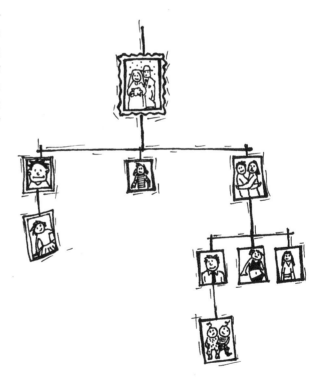

Over the years, you may like to look at a few sentences from the Bible that tell us that we should not fear death. Here are one or two:

> *The souls of the upright are in the hands of God and no torment can touch them.*
>
> The Book of Wisdom 3.1[1]

> *... I am certain that nothing can separate us from his love: neither death nor life, neither angels nor other heavenly rulers or powers, neither the present nor the future, neither the world above nor the world below – there is nothing in all creation that will ever be able to separate us from the love of God which is ours through Christ Jesus.*
>
> Romans 8.38-39 (GNB)

> *'Now God's home is with human beings! He will live with them, and they shall be his people. God himself will be with them, and he will be their God. He will wipe away all tears from their eyes. There will be no more death, no more grief or crying or pain. The old things have disappeared.'*
>
> Revelation 21.3-4 (The Vision of the Heavenly Jerusalem) (GNB)

A Prayer for All Souls Day

Eternal God, we thank you for all those we have remembered today.
Let your wonderful light shine on them for ever, Lord, and may they always rest in peace. Amen.

1.The Book of Wisdom will not be found in all Bibles. It is part of the Apocrypha, which contains extra books not included in all versions of the Old Testament. Nevertheless, it contains some very beautiful writing and is worth looking out for.

Firework fun and the Catherine Wheel: November

November is bonfire month and you will almost certainly see some fireworks one way or another. Perhaps one of the best known named fireworks is the Catherine Wheel, so you might use a visit to a firework display as an excuse to remember the story of brave St Catherine, and to pray for people who are prepared to speak about Jesus in difficult situations today.

Catherine lived in Egypt when it was part of the Roman Empire. She was a young Christian from an influential family who, having confronted the pagan emperor, was invited to debate the cause of Christianity with leading teachers. When she won the debate, the Emperor ordered that she be tortured to death, by being crushed by wheels covered in saw blades and nails. The wheels, however, fell to pieces and she was spared. As a result of this, more people became Christians. Catherine was finally beheaded, but she has never been forgotten.

In England, firework displays are usually around 5 November. St Catherine's Day is 25 November. If you buy your own fireworks, you could save a Catherine Wheel for 25 November. If you attend a big firework display, you could remember Catherine, and the people she reminds us to pray for, before you set out.

Praying with St Catherine

On a piece of paper, draw a wheel with a hub in the middle and eight spokes. Think of some people who have spoken out bravely about the Christian life and write their names along some of the spokes. Think of some places where you need to be very brave to speak out as a Christian and write these along the other spokes. Draw a cross on the wheel hub. Very simply, thank God for people who have been brave enough to speak out for Jesus, and pray for people in places where it is hard to be a Christian.

St Martin's Day: 11 November

Now that you have started wearing warm clothes again, you might like to spend a bit of time sorting out clothes that have been outgrown or are no longer worn, but are still in good condition. There may be someone to pass them on to. If not, you may like to take them to a charity shop.

Then you could share the story of St Martin of Tours, the patron saint of France, who is remembered on 11 November.

Martin was born in the fourth century in the country of Hungary but became an important Roman soldier in France. One cold winter day in the town of Amiens, he met a beggar in the street who had no clothes at all. Martin was so sorry for him that he cut his own cloak in half and gave half of it to the beggar. This helped him to understand that God didn't want him to fight but to care for people, so he gave up being a soldier and became a priest instead. He worked as a priest in Poitiers and built the first monastery in France, at Liguge. After that he was made Bishop of Tours on the river Loire.

You could find a map of France and identify the places associated with St Martin

Read the Bible

The story in St Matthew's Gospel, chapter 25, verses 34 to 40 is one which St Martin would have understood well. Perhaps you might like to read it.

I was hungry and you fed me, thirsty and you gave me a drink; I was a stranger and you received me in your homes, naked and you clothed me.

Matthew 25.35-36 (GNB)

A Prayer

Help us to share Lord,
and make us always aware of the needs of others
and ready to respond. Amen.

46

Make the journey: the beginning of Advent

If you have a Christmas crib set, get it out on Advent Sunday (four Sundays before Christmas Day) and give it a clean-up together. Then decide where you will set it up. Put the stable and the empty manger there, and one animal. Spread the rest of the figures around different parts of the house: Mary and Joseph in one room, the shepherds and their sheep in another. Replace the kings in the box and put them away until Christmas itself and put the baby in a special, safe hiding place, close to the stable.

Every day, between now and Christmas, Mary and Joseph can travel a little closer to the stable. The sheep can follow the shepherds, moving closer to the stable also.

On the day before Christmas Eve, Mary and Joseph will reach the stable and the shepherds will be nearby. On Christmas Eve, put the baby in the manger and on Christmas Day, put the shepherds in the stable. On Christmas Day, the kings start their journey from another room to the stable, arriving on 6 January.

'Be on the alert and pray always that you will have the strength to go safely through all those things that will happen and to stand before the Son of Man.'

Luke 21.36 (GNB)

An Advent Prayer

Say this prayer as you move the figures

Lord Jesus, light of the world,
Born in David's city of Bethlehem,
Born like him to be a king:
Be born in our hearts this Christmastide,
Be king of our lives today. Amen.

(from *The Promise of His Glory*, p. 137)

47

Advent angels

Cover a board with dark blue paper. Using the template, draw 25 angels on gold and silver wrapping paper and cut them out. Cut 25 little pieces of paper too, one for each angel to carry. Put the angels and the papers in an envelope or special box near the board.

Each day in Advent, one member of the family sticks an angel on the board. When the angel has been stuck on, someone writes a short prayer on one of the little pieces of paper and then reads it out.

At the end everyone says:

> Come Lord Jesus,
>
> *Come to your waiting world.*

Then roll up the little piece of paper to make a scroll and stick it on the angel's hands.

Prayers

In Advent we pray for the world to become a fit place for Jesus when he comes in glory. Here are some ideas for the prayers the angels will hold:

> **Pray . . .**
> **for people who love us,**
> **for peace in the world,**
> **for people who are sad or scared,**
> **for rulers,**
> **for ourselves as we get ready for Jesus to come.**

Secrets with St Nicholas:
6 December

On 6 December, we remember St Nicholas. He was a bishop who lived in Turkey in the fourth century and specialized in rescuing young people in distress. He is said to have thrown three sacks of gold through the window of a poor man about to sell his daughters into slavery, rescued three young boys who were kidnapped and pickled by a wicked innkeeper, and begged for food from the grain ships for the starving people in his city of Myra. These legends have been the inspiration for some special customs on St Nicholas Day.

In Germany, Holland and Belgium people make special St Nicholas biscuits. Use the recipe to make your own. Another custom is giving presents very secretly, as St Nicholas did when he threw the gold through the window into the poor man's house. Why not make some biscuits today and see if you can give them away to someone without them knowing where they have come from? (This could involve an expedition to a neighbour's house under cover of darkness.) Very little people may need to check in a few days' time, to make sure that the biscuits were found!

How to make St Nicholas biscuits

200g (8oz) plain flour
1tsp baking powder
100g (4oz) margarine
150g (6oz) sugar
1 beaten egg
cinnamon, ginger and allspice to taste

Rub the fat into the flour, add the sugar, spices and mix with the egg. Chill the mixture a little then roll it out. Cut it into circles to make St Nicholas faces. Add eyes using sultanas and make a mouth with bits of cherry. You could press some leftover bits of mixture through a garlic press to make the beard. Finally make a triangle to go on top to make a bishop's hat (often called a mitre) and put a cross on this. (Or you could roll the mixture into a sausage shape and just cut it into round slices.) Bake it at 190°C (Gas Mark 5) for 5 to 10 minutes.

The Sovereign Lord has filled me with his Spirit. He has chosen me and sent me to bring good news to the poor, to heal the broken-hearted, to announce release to captives and freedom to those in prison.

Isaiah 61.1 (GNB)

49

Putting up the Christmas Tree

Don't put your tree up too early. The anticipation can be just as exciting as having the tree up, so build on this. The tree can be prepared in stages, to make the waiting more active and more fun: buy it one day, pot it another. Leave it outside and water it well so that the needles stay fresh. With an artificial tree get it out, take it outside and dust it down.

If you have lights on your tree, a grown-up will need to check in good time that all the bulbs still work. If you need some new ones, check the fitting and enjoy the trip out to buy them: children can be involved in even the most ordinary jobs. Set some time aside so that you can enjoy putting the tree up together.

Make sure you have some particularly Christian decorations on your tree along with the other baubles:

✳ You could make beautiful stars out of foil and glitter.

✳ You can buy lovely straw or string angels in charity shops.

✳ Bells remind us of the Church.

✳ You could make a tiny cradle for baby Jesus out of half a walnut shell and a little bit of white cloth or bandage.

Cover the pot or bucket that holds your tree with coloured paper and then stick on this beautiful message, which is based on some words in the Bible:

> 'Then shall all the trees of the forest sing for joy before the Lord; for he is coming...'

Psalm 96.12-13 (NRSV)

Older children may like to make a new sign each year. You could make it on a computer if you have one. You can stick the paper sign onto foil or gold wrapping paper so that it has a shiny edge.

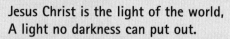

Prayers

When the tree is all ready, you could say this prayer together:

Lord, bless our Christmas tree,
a sign which we have decorated with fruits
of the earth and with lights.
Help us to shine as lights in the world. Amen.

And you could use one of these short prayers each day as you switch on the tree lights:

Jesus Christ is the light of the world,
A light no darkness can put out.

The shepherds kept watch by night,
And your glory shone round about them.

Lord, the darkness is not dark to you,
The night is as bright as the day.

Lord, let your light scatter the darkness
And fill the church with your glory.

(all from *The Promise of His Glory*, p. 165)

General

Bedtime prayers

Here are some little prayers to use at bedtime:

> Glory to thee my God, this night,
> For all the blessings of the light.
> Keep me, O keep me, King of kings
> Beneath thy own almighty wings. Amen.
>
> Thomas Ken (1637–1711)

> Dear Jesus, please be with me
> From now until the end.
> Hold my hand and guide my feet
> And be my special friend. Amen.
>
> (from Joan Gale Thomas,
> *If I'd Been Born in Bethlehem.*)

Save us O Lord, while waking,
And guard us while sleeping.
That awake we may watch with Christ
And asleep we may rest in peace. Amen.

God in the night
God at my right
God all the day
God with me stay
God in my heart
Never depart
God with thy might
Keep us in light
Through this dark night

(From David Adam, *The Edge of Glory: Prayers in the Celtic Tradition*, p. 38)

Keep us safe tonight Lord;
May your angels watch over us.
And tomorrow, help us to be angels,
Bringing your love to anyone who
needs help. Amen.

Rhyming prayers are particularly good to use with very small children who soon learn to say the last word of every other line. Then before you know it, they can say the whole prayer off by heart. Simple prayers like this, learnt off by heart when we are very small, are with us for ever, whenever we need them. Though we may learn other ways of being close to God as we grow older, these prayers are a firm foundation on which to build.

Some good books to look out for

Children's Bibles

The Dorling Kindersley *Illustrated Children's Bible* has the most important stories retold with wonderful illustrations and helpful snippets of background information.

The Dorling Kindersley *Illustrated Family Bible* is a bit bigger and uses passages from the Bible itself rather than retelling the stories.

The Jerusalem Bible for Children (published by Darton, Longman and Todd) also uses Bible passages to tell the most important stories.

The Lion First Bible (published by Lion)

A Pocketful of Stories (published by Lion)

Books of Bible stories and stories which explain the Bible

The Teddy Horsley books (published by the National Christian Education Council) are very small books, ideal for children under seven. They explore ideas from the Bible very simply.

The Bible story books by Nick Butterworth and Nick Inkpen are very enjoyable. Look out for all of them – *The Little Gate, The Rich Farmer, The Precious Pearl* and many more. They are published by Marshall Pickering and include a teeny version. Two other sets of tiny books are *The Story of Jesus Library*: eight small books in a box published by Hodder and Stoughton and the Lion *Treasure Chest* series.

Books of Prayers

Nightlights: four books to help two to six year olds to pray. *(Safe this Night, Bright Star Night, All Year Long, Sad News, Glad News.)* Published by Lion.

Little Prayers Series: *Mealtime Prayers, Bedtime Prayers, Prayers of Praise, Classic Children's Prayers.* Published by Hunt and Thorpe.

The Lord's Prayer: The Prayer that Jesus Taught Two Thousand Years Ago. An explanation by Lois Rock. Published by Lion.

It's a Big Family! The Lord's Prayer for Young Readers by Brian Ogden. Published by the Bible Reading Fellowship.

Praying Through Life: How to Pray in the Home, at Work and in the Family. A book about learning to pray which would be good for any family, by Stephen Cottrell. Published by the National Society and Church House Publishing.

Some other books

The Curious History of God by Russell Stannard, published by Lion. A book for older children about the big questions people asked, how the Bible has explored them and how people still explore them today. Russell Stannard is a well-known scientist and a Christian writer.

A Feast of Good Stories by Pat Alexander, published by Lion. Lots of stories by different writers gathered together because they express the values 'that our world needs'.

Song of the Morning: Easter Stories and Poems for Children, also by Pat Alexander and published by Lion

Famous prayers

There are probably as many ways to pray as there are people of faith. Sometimes it is helpful just to be still and aware of God with us, sometimes it is helpful to do something to remind us that God is with us and sometimes it is helpful to pray with words. Some prayers we read and some we know off by heart because we have heard others say them so many times. In the past, in a world where few people could read, learning prayers off by heart was really important. Here are a few prayers, which people have known and used for centuries, which have passed the test of time and still help us to be close to God today. Choose one to say together from time to time, and soon you will all know it. Some were written by famous people; no one knows where others came from.

The Prayer of St Francis

Lord, make me an instrument of your peace;
where there is hatred, let me sow love;
where there is injury, pardon;
where there is discord, union;
where there is doubt, faith;
where there is despair, hope;
where there is darkness, light;
where there is sadness, joy;
for your mercy and for your truth's sake. Amen.

We praise you, O Christ,
and we bless you,
because by your holy cross
you have redeemed the world. Amen.

Thou who hast given so much to me,
give one thing more,
a grateful heart,
for Christ's sake. Amen.

George Herbert (1593-1632)

Christ has no body now on earth but yours,
no hands but yours, no feet but yours;
yours are the eyes through which to look
at Christ's compassion to the world,
yours are the feet
with which he is to go about doing good,
and yours are the hands
with which he is to bless us now. Amen.

St Teresa of Avila (1515-1582)

O Lord, thou knowest how busy I must be this day;
if I forget thee, do not thou forget me;
for Christ's sake. Amen.

General Lord Astley's prayer before the Battle of Edge Hill.
He lived from 1579 to 1652.

O Lord, let us not live to be useless,
for Christ's sake. Amen.

John Wesley (1703-1791)

Teach us, good Lord, to serve thee as thou deservest.
To give and not to count the cost;
to fight and not to heed the wounds;
to toil and not to seek for rest;
to labour and not to ask for any reward
save that of knowing that we do thy will. Amen.

Ignatius Loyola (1491-1556)

Thanks be to thee,
O Lord Jesus Christ,
for all the benefits which thou hast won for us,
for all the pains and insults which thou hast borne for us.
O most merciful Redeemer,
Friend and Brother,
may we know thee more clearly,
love thee more dearly,
and follow thee more nearly,
day by day. Amen.

St Richard of Chichester (1197-1253)

53

Being still

In all the rush and noise of our busy lives, it is easy never to be still and quiet. We hear what other people think from the TV and the radio, from disks and tapes and videos, but often we don't have time even to think about what we think, let alone talk about it! And we certainly don't have time to think about or listen to God. Christians have always known that one way to be aware of God, to be close to God, is in being still, in silence. Even tiny children can do this for a few minutes and it can be a great experience to try it out.

If it's possible, choose a time when you can be just one grown-up and one child together. Most children need to be at least three to try this, but it's better to begin when they are small. And choose a time when you can be sure there won't be lots of interruptions. In summer time, you could go out to a quiet place, a garden or park, a walk beside the canal or river or into a cemetery or churchyard. Find a place to sit down together and agree that you are both going to be very still and completely silent for an agreed time. (The length of time depends very much on the age of the child and whether or not you have done this before.) You might like to start with being still for half a minute; you may even be able to manage a minute.

So sit together and agree to be still. Close your eyes together (though you may need to promise to keep an eye on the watch too!) and, keeping close together, be silent. When sufficient time has passed, open your eyes and talk about how it was in the silence.

    *   How was the silence for you?

    *   What did you hear?

    *   What did you smell?

    *   What did you feel?

    *   What did you imagine?

Share together what you found.

Be still and know that I am God.

Psalm 46.10 (NRSV)

A Prayer

Here's a prayer you might like to use. It is quite a grown-up prayer in some ways, but if you say it often with a little child, he or she will learn it off by heart and then it will be there whenever it is needed.

Drop thy still dews of quietness
till all our strivings cease;
take from our souls the strain and stress
and let our ordered lives confess
the beauty of thy peace. Amen.

John Greenleaf Whittier (1807-92)

Saying grace

From earliest times, people have thanked God for their food and for all that kept them alive. In our lives today, it is all too easy to take everyday things for granted. To stop and say thank you for them helps us to be aware of the very basics of survival, and that without God's love and generosity, we should not be. When we do this, we, in turn become much more closely aware of the needs of others and of those who have so little, and we learn to become more generous people. So before you eat, at least sometimes, stop. And say THANK YOU.

Here is a selection of short thank-you prayers, to be said before eating. Most can be said by anyone and it is important that you share round the responsibility – or choose one prayer to say all together often.

> For these and all God's gifts, may his name be praised. Amen.

> Blessed are You, Lord our God, King of the universe,
> who feeds the whole world through His goodness. Amen.

If you like singing, you could find a tune to which you could sing the following words.

But if you don't sing, you can still say them.

> Praise God, from whom all blessings flow,
> Praise Him, all creatures, here below.
> Praise Him above, ye heavenly host.
> Praise Father, Son and Holy Ghost. Amen.

> God bless this bunch
> As they munch their lunch. Amen.

A grace to be said when you share a meal with friends

For good food, and good friends
we thank you Lord. Amen.

Lord, all living things look hopefully to you,
and you give them food when they need it.
You give them enough
and satisfy the needs of all.

From Psalm 145 (NRSV)

If you are having visitors children might like to make little cards with the words of a grace prayer on them so that everyone can join in together.

The Lord's Prayer

Jesus' disciples asked him to teach them to pray and he gave them the prayer we have come to know as the Lord's Prayer. It is said by Christians throughout the world, and of course, in many different languages. It is a prayer that all Christian people should know. In two places in the Bible you can read about how Jesus taught it to his disciples. Look in St Matthew's Gospel, chapter 6, verses 5 to 13 and in St Luke's Gospel, chapter 11, verses 2 to 4. Jesus, of course, taught it to his disciples in their own language and this has been translated into English in various ways at various times. There are two versions given here: the most recent text, agreed by English-speaking Christians across the world, and the older English text written at about the time the Bible was first translated into English.

Try to say it at some time every day.

Our Father in heaven,
hallowed be your Name,
your kingdom come,
your will be done
on earth as it is in heaven.
Give us today our daily bread.
Forgive us our sins
as we forgive those who sin against us.
Save us from the time of trial
and deliver us from evil.
For the kingdom, the power
and the glory are yours,
now and for ever. Amen.

Our Father, which art in heaven,
hallowed be thy name;
thy kingdom come;
thy will be done;
in earth as it is in heaven.
Give us this day our daily bread;
And forgive us our trespasses,
as we forgive them that trespass against us.
And lead us not into temptation,
but deliver us from evil.
For thine is the kingdom,
the power, and the glory,
for ever and ever. Amen.

Children and God: talking about God with children

Pre-schoolers

Pre-school children are often instinctively aware of God and will talk about God quite naturally. Sometimes they give breathtaking descriptions of their experiences of God, sometimes they ask questions, often they point things out to us. It is important to have these conversations and delight in them. Small children love to play with ideas, with images and symbols: they collect and treasure experiences, just as they collect and treasure things. Our job, as adults who love and care for them, is to share and delight in these experiences with our children. By the time we spend, the outings we provide, the toys and playthings we offer, we are able to enrich the experiences and opportunities that are available. We don't need to know all the answers, to provide watertight explanations or convey complicated doctrines. All those things can wait until much, much later.

Tiny children learn through exploration and experience: this is as true of their know ledge of God as it is with anything else. It is in being held close as you say a prayer together, or sing 'Alleluia' in church or look at the stars, or as you hunt for shells, or play a game or listen to a story, that a little child soaks up and treasures the wonder that is God. They may not be able to explain complicated ideas with long words, but their experience of God is nevertheless vibrant and exciting. We must rejoice and delight in that and encourage others to do so. There is plenty of time for complicated explanations later in life.

Primary school children

As children progress through school, stories and questions become more important. They enjoy longer and more complex stories; facts, and questions and answers become paramount, though the opportunities to undertake practical tasks and burn

off energy remain of great importance. School age children are usually busy, and it is important to ensure that there is time for God in all this busyness. Simple tasks that mark important days, the chance to talk as adults and children together about what is really important to us and the opportunity to encounter endless stories will help to nurture an awareness of God who is close to us, who sustains us but gives us the freedom to explore and discover.

This is the time when children may start to ask questions which intimidate us. Just be honest. Faith is about life's big questions. The quest for God is a lifetime's work. Even the most important Christians constantly face doubts and questions. Talk together about questions raised and explore ideas: complicated questions do not have simple answers. And look for books and other people to help. The very best Children's Bibles now available usually have all sorts of helpful background information included on each page to help in exploring Bible stories, and the church should be full of people who can help us to explore other questions. Maybe if adults asked as many questions as children do we would be a livelier and more vibrant community!

Source list

David Adam, *The Edge of Glory: Prayers in the Celtic Tradition*, Triangle/SPCK, 1985

Eric Carle, *The Very Hungry Caterpillar*, Puffin, 1974

Common Worship: Initiation Services, Church House Publishing, 1998

Common Worship: Services and Prayers for the Church of England, Church House Publishing, 2000

Christopher Herbert, compiler, *Prayers for Children*, Church House Publishing, 1993

Angela Elwell Hunt, *The Tale of Three Trees*, Lion, 1989

Lent, Holy Week, Easter: Services and Prayers, Church House Publishing/SPCK, 1984, 1986

The Promise of His Glory: Services and Prayers for the Season from All Saints to Candlemas, Church House Publishing, 1990, 1991

Joan Gale Thomas, *If I'd Been Born in Bethlehem*, Mowbray, 1958